Bou

written by Pam Holden
illustrated by Pauline Whimp

1

As the chilly winter brought the first heavy snowfalls, the black bears began to move into sheltered dens in caves or hollow tree stumps to hibernate. A fat glossy female bear entered her den in a cave, where she had prepared a nest lined with pine branches and leaves. When the freezing winter winds blew, she settled down to sleep for many weeks until her three tiny blind cubs were born.

To keep warm they snuggled together in the mother bear's thick fur, while she fed them with her own nourishing milk. As they grew, their eyes opened and they started exploring their home in the snug, sheltered cave. They developed into chubby little balls of fur, romping like playful puppies, tumbling and pouncing on each other.

Once the bitterly cold winter was over, everything began to thaw. The mother bear led her three cubs outside the den to learn about their environment. She taught them how to search for food so they would no longer need to drink her milk. They wandered through the woods feasting on delicious berries and tender shoots, climbing trees to find honey, and swimming in the lake to catch fish. As they became more and more independent, the mother bear watched them carefully to guard them from danger. She worried most about the biggest cub, Bouncer, who did naughty things like running away and hiding behind bushes.

4

One day Bouncer's mischief caused terrible trouble, because he
wandered far away from his family until he found a huge pile of
garbage. He was busily rummaging through food scraps, feeling
very clever to have found such an exciting heap of nice food,
when he smelt something delicious. So he nosed through layers
of garbage, following the scent right into a large plastic jar.
He reached in to gobble a piece of tasty fish from the bottom
of the jar, but he couldn't pull his head back out again!
The cub was trapped tight with his head deep inside a jar!

Poor Bouncer was a prisoner! He began to panic, jumping frantically about in an attempt to dislodge the jar. Shaking his head didn't help at all, so he tried pushing at the rim of the jar with his claws, but it was stuck firmly. Pulling back with the jar against the edge of a sharp rock didn't work either, while rolling on the ground seemed to make the jar tighter still!

The frightened cub couldn't roar out to the other bears, but luckily he managed to see them through the clear plastic, so he bounded back to join them. When they saw what had happened to Bouncer, the worried bears knew that he was in serious danger, unable to eat or drink. He had got himself into a life-threatening situation! There was not a single thing his family could do to rescue him.

A fortunate thing happened the next day, when some hikers in the forest saw the bear family and were aware that the trapped cub couldn't possibly survive without skilled help. They called the wildlife rangers to report the problem, so a team of experts immediately hurried into the vast forest to hunt for the unlucky young bear.

Some special traps were quickly set with tasty bait to lure the hungry bears, but that trick failed to tempt them. Every day during the next week, the rangers received new messages from groups of hikers reporting where the bears had been seen, but it seemed impossible to track them down in time before they moved further away.

By the tenth day the searchers were giving up hope, believing there was no chance of success after such a length of time. Just when everyone thought that poor Bouncer had been trapped without food or water for too long to survive, their luck changed. The rangers observed the mother bear feasting on berries quite close by! They carefully shot a special dart into her side, sending her immediately into a deep sleep. She was moved into a holding cage while they searched urgently for Bouncer.

He was soon spotted, tackled, and wrestled to the ground, still struggling weakly to escape his rescuers. The battered plastic jar was carefully pulled off his head before he was taken to the cage. Poor starving Bouncer couldn't wait for his mother to wake, so he fed greedily from her while she slept.

18

His brother and sister were much more difficult to catch – they bounded through the woods, dodging behind bushes as they tried to escape. But the skilled rangers finally had all three cubs locked safely in the cage where their sedated mother lay sleeping soundly. The wildlife team watched the bear family closely all day and through the night to check two important developments:
- that Bouncer was feeding; and
- that his mother had woken.

Early the next day, their cage was taken on a trailer deep into
the forest, where the doors suddenly clanged open as the whole
family was released. Bouncer was the first one out, zooming like
a rocket, with the other three bears following at high speed. They
were so relieved, happy to be back where they belonged, far away
from people and garbage.

Bouncer had finally learned a vital lesson of survival – to stay
near his mother and family, and keep away from trouble.

NEWS

The News

'Jarhead' bear gets out of a jam in Florida

The cub was in a life-threatening situation because it could not eat or drink

A bear cub in Florida, which had a plastic jar stuck on its head for at least 10 days, has now been freed.

The cub, affectionately nicknamed "Jarhead", got its head stuck in the container while rooting through rubbish around the town of Weirsdale.

The cub was days away from death as he had not been able to eat or drink, biologists who rescued the bear said.

They sedated the mother bear before grabbing the cub, pinning his ears back and with much pushing and pulling, finally removed the container.

Jarhead Bear Re-Released Into Wild

The bear cub and his entire family were re-released into a less populated forest for their own safety.

NEWS

EXTRA!

'Jarhead' bear gets out of a jam in Florida

The cub was in a life-threatening situation because it could not eat or drink

A bear cub in Florida, which had a plastic jar stuck on its head for at least 10 days, has now been freed.

The cub, affectionately nicknamed "Jarhead", got its head stuck in the container while rooting through rubbish around the town of Weirsdale.

The cub was days away from death as he had not been able to eat or drink, biologists who rescued the bear said.

They sedated the mother bear before grabbing the cub, pinning his ears back and with much pushing and pulling, finally removed the container.

Jarhead Bear Re-Released Into Wild

The bear cub and his entire family were re-released into a less populated forest for their own safety.

NEWS